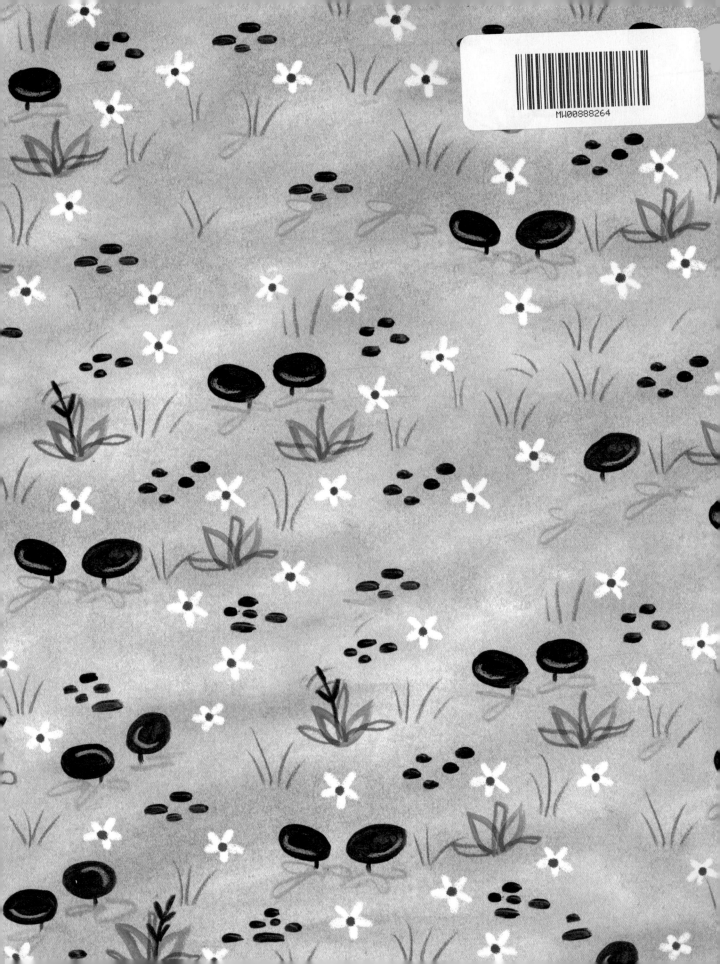

Dedicated to all the lovely children in my family

What is self-care?

Self-care means caring for yourself. Washing your hands, brushing your teeth, learning new things, and playing with friends are some examples. Self-care means making sure our minds and bodies are healthy. There are many different ways to use self-care. We'll show you more in this book!

www.mascotbooks.com

Self-Care with Ted and Friends

For more information, please contact:
Mascot Books
620 Herndon Parkway, Suite 320
Herndon, VA 20170
info@mascotbooks.com

Library of Congress Control Number: 2021916643

CPSIA Code: PRT0921A
ISBN-13: 978-1-64543-997-4

Printed in the United States

Self-Care
with Ted and Friends

Najma Khorrami

Illustrated by Maria Ballarin

Hi, guys, my name is Ted. My friends and I play, eat, sleep, and are kind to one another . . .

We like to care for ourselves,
which means we use self-care.

We are flying a kite.
We love flying our kite!
Ahh! It is super windy for Ted, but it is still fun!

Flying a kite can be a challenge, but trying is the important part. Trying is so, so important.

We are playing tag.
We love tag!
Ahh! Shawn is it! Come and tag me, Shawn!

1-2-3-4-5-6-7-8-9-10!
Here I come! Ready or not!

We are playing hide-and-seek.
We love hide-and-seek!
It is so much fun, and we love to giggle,
especially with Shelly the bunny.

Laughing out loud helps us forget about
being bored or upset.
It lifts our mood and makes us happy.

We are finding some leaves, nuts, and berries.
They help some of us, like Shawn
the caterpillar and Luis the squirrel, grow bigger.

Taking care of our bodies is important and
helps the mind.

We are running around in the forest.
Yippy! We love to run around, especially with each other.

Ted gets along well with his friends.
He likes to surround himself with others who care for him and enjoy his company.

We are taking our time.
We love taking our time to do great things,
like building a tree house.

Being patient is a cure for so many things.
It helps us feel better, too.

We are talking now.
We love talking!
You're so nice, Shelly, for listening!

It always helps Ted to share his feelings
with someone he trusts,
like Shelly the bunny.

We are taking a nap.
We love taking a nap!
Zzz . . .

Getting good rest, especially at night,
is good for the mind.
We feel better with rest, too.

We are catching fireflies in the night.
We love catching fireflies!
Whoa! Look how many of them are out!

We have a great passion to catch fireflies.
It even lets our hands glow!
We love to glow bright.

We are letting the fireflies go now.
We love letting them go!
Christina, we promise we will let them all free!

It is a great trait to let things go, especially fireflies.
If you don't need to hold on to things,
letting go is also good for the mind.

We are learning at home.
We love learning!
Look at us count and do math!

Learning helps the mind grow.
It helps us explore our surroundings and
expand our knowledge.

We are sharing what we appreciate about
our friends: Ted, Shawn, Luis, Christina, and Shelly.
We love saying thanks!

Expressing our gratitude helps keep the mind
happy and strong.

Enjoying the weather is the best for
Ted's self-care.

THE END

About the Author

Najma Khorrami founded her company, Gratitude Circle®, in 2017. Najma grew up in Centreville, Virginia, where she attended Centreville High School and had many great teachers. She attended The George Washington University, where she also earned a master's degree in public health. She loves all kinds of art, including photography and painting. Najma was inspired to write *Self-Care with Ted and Friends* because of her joyous childhood, including her stuffed animal bear, Ted, which all her family knows she loved. Najma can't wait to make new memories with all the children and families who learn about self-care through this book!